W9-CYV-637

The Sinking of
CAPTAIN OTTER

Withdrawn

Written by
Troy Wilson

Illustrated by
Maira Chiodi

Owlkids Books

Batavia Public Library
Batavia, Illinois

Kelpy was a captain.
He had the heart for it.
The head for it.
The hat for it.

And after a whole
lot of building...

...he had the ship for it, too!

All of the other otters laughed,

and laughed,

and laughed.

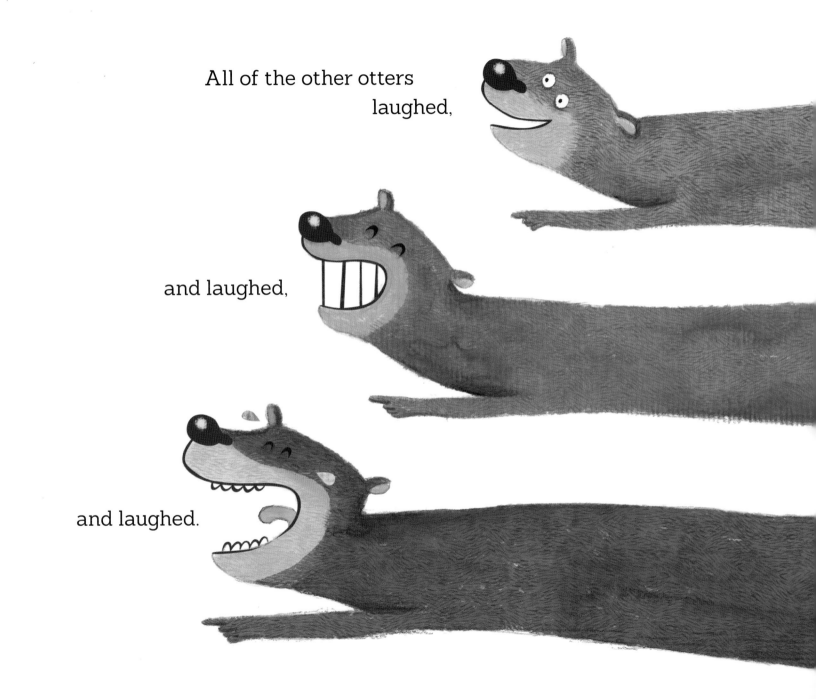

Kelpy sighed a little.
He cried a little.
But he loved his ship.
He loved her from keel
        to cabin
            to crow's nest.

So he took a deep breath,
straightened his hat,
and sailed on.

Pirates...
    laughed.

Sharks...
     laughed.

Har
Har
Har
Har
Har
Har

Even the waves...
laughed,
and laughed,
and laughed.

Kelpy sighed a little.
He cried a little.
But he loved his ship.
He loved her from keel
    to cabin
        to crow's nest.

So he took a deep breath,
straightened his hat,
and sailed on.

Pirates.
Again.

"Arrr!" came a shout.
"I be Blistering Blastering Butterbeard.
Prepare to be sunk!"

Kelpy laughed,
   and laughed,
      and laughed.

Butterbeard sighed a little.
He cried a little.

And a little more.

And a little more.

Actually...
he cried A LOT.

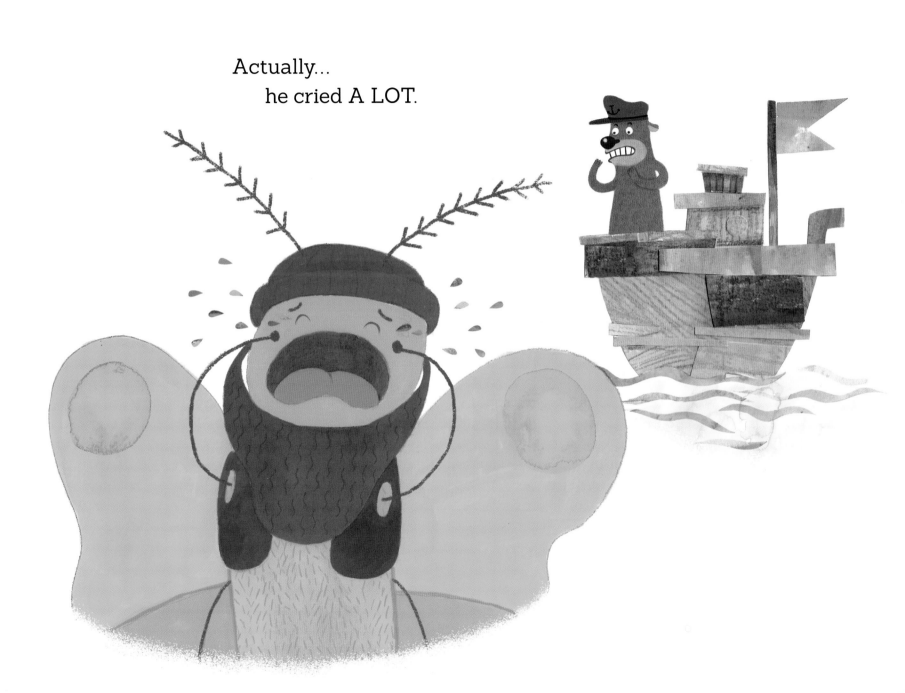

Kelpy loved his ship.
He loved her from keel
    to cabin
        to crow's nest.

But...
he knew what he had to do.
He knew in his head.
He knew in his heart.

So he took a deep breath,
readied his axe,
and swung on.

CHIP,
CHAP,
CHOP!

"Oh, no!" cried Kelpy.
"Your cannonball smashed my ship!"

"I'm sinking!"

"I'm s-i-i-i-n-k i i i i n g !"

"Hah!" roared Butterbeard.
"Let that be a lesson to ye!"

"Let that be a lesson to all who sail the same ocean as Blistering Blastering Butterbeard!"

"If I could, I'd sink ye a million times!"

"Nay, a billion!
Nay, a trillion!"

"Oh, yeah?" said Kelpy. "I dare you to!"

"*Ye*. Dare. *Me?!*" hissed Butterbeard.

"I double-dog dare you! Triple-dog dare!
Quadruple-dog, sea-dog dare!"

And with that,
they knew what they had to do.
Their hearts were in it.
Their heads were in it.
Their hats were in it.

And after a whole lot of rebuilding...

...their ships were back in it, too!

So they bellowed their bluster,
straightened their aims,
and sunk on.

A million,

a billion,

a trillion times.

And they laughed,

and laughed,

and laughed.

To Mrs. Eivindson for assigning,
praising, and reading aloud the
original version of *Captain Otter*
at John Howitt Elementary in
Port Alberni, BC.

And to my six-year-old self for
writing and illustrating it — T.W.

For my family — M.C.

Text © 2018 Troy Wilson
Illustrations © 2018 Maira Chiodi

All rights reserved. No part of this publication may be reproduced,
stored in a retrieval system, or transmitted in any form or by any means,
without the prior written permission of Owlkids Books Inc., or in the
case of photocopying or other reprographic copying, a license from the
Canadian Copyright Licensing Agency (Access Copyright). For an Access
Copyright license, visit www.accesscopyright.ca or call toll-free to
1-800-893-5777.

Owlkids Books acknowledges the financial support of the Canada
Council for the Arts, the Ontario Arts Council, the Government of
Canada through the Canada Book Fund (CBF) and the Government of
Ontario through the Ontario Media Development Corporation's Book
Initiative for our publishing activities.

Published in Canada by
Owlkids Books Inc.
10 Lower Spadina Avenue
Toronto, ON M5V 2Z2

Published in the United States by
Owlkids Books Inc.
1700 Fourth Street
Berkeley, CA 94710

Library of Congress Control Number: 2017961366

Library and Archives Canada Cataloguing in Publication

Wilson, Troy, 1970-, author
    The sinking of Captain Otter / Troy Wilson ; illustrated by Maira Chiodi.

ISBN 978-1-77147-311-8 (hardcover)
    I. Chiodi, Maira, illustrator II. Title.

PS8645.I48S56 2018   jC813'.6   C2017-907437-7

Edited by: Debbie Rogosin
Designed by: Danielle Arbour and Alisa Baldwin

Manufactured in Shenzhen, Guangdong, China, in April 2018, by WKT Co. Ltd.
Job #17CB2759

A   B   C   D   E   F